The Elephant and the Dragon:
A Fable

Of The Fable Triad

CS Simpson

Published by CSS Stories, 2022

Written by CS Simpson
Cover design by CS Simpson
Inside illustrations by Pierre Gregory
Published by CSS Stories, CS Simpson's self-publishing line

ISBN: 9798201791537

For my parents, Greg and Anne

Thank you for your unwavering support

"The worst loneliness is to not be comfortable with yourself."

~ Mark Twain

"A fair-minded person tries to see both sides of an argument."

~ Aesop

TABLE OF CONTENTS

STORY INTRODUCTION

CREATED FOR ALL READERS, *The Elephant and the Dragon* is a new tale told in an old writing style. I grew up with a copy of Rudyard Kipling's *Just So Stories* (from 1902) and was fascinated by his strange accounts of the supposed origins of unusual creatures and language, talking animals in a non picture book, and his clever use of language to make an important point. I wrote this story with the idea of creating a similarly timeless tale and to remind us all of the need for social courtesy in a gentle way.

In order to set the fable apart from most commercial stories, I've chosen to write my fables with an intentional lack of contractions, as well as deliberate repetitions of both phrases and ideas. These repetitions are meant to draw the reader into an ancient kind of suspended reality, reinforce a concept, and even give the story its own poetic rhythm.

Likewise, I chose the intentional use of lists in sets of threes, including the final tally of this book series—The

Fable Triad. Many cultures revere triads because they're seen as having a beginning, a middle, and an end—creating a sense of completeness.

I was fortunate to grow up near the San Diego Zoo and fell in love with animals of all species at an early age. I decided to name each character based on the area of the globe where scientists think these creatures may have originated, and I've included a pronunciation guide at the back of the book for those who are interested. The tale is set "a very long time ago, before there were many people roaming the Earth," so the intention is meant to show (perhaps) that mankind adopted these names, with the character's dominating personalities, into their respective languages over time. It's also meant to show how immense and varied our world is, yet we all have a common beginning; a common existence; body, mind, and spirit.

My fables are unique in that they each have several morals interwoven within the narrative, instead of the classic idea of ending the story with a single, intended teaching. The lessons represented in these stories are age-old, yet still timely for every culture.

Though each of my fables are separate tales with separate characters, they're meant to embody the same global time frame and can be read in any order. They begin almost identically, much like Kipling's *Just So*

Stories, in order to set the tone and rhythm as complementary to the other two. But—worry not! *The Elephant and the Dragon, The Dolphin and the Octopus,* and *The Mermaid and the River Otter*, each offer their own unique accounts and don't follow the exact same pattern throughout.

I welcome readers of any age and even hope that parents think of this story as a family book— perhaps one to be read aloud and discussed together.

Enjoy!

– CS Simpson

CHAPTER 1

A VERY LONG TIME AGO, BEFORE THERE were many people roaming the Earth, an elephant and a dragon guided The Animal Kingdom together in a protected valley high in the mountains. Both governors were wise, kind, and gentle souls who made an effort to counsel the many creatures of the land and air without prejudice. Being trusted to manage others was a very great responsibility, so they held this power very carefully.

The ash gray female elephant, named Ujuzi (which means "experience, knowledge" in Swahili), was known as The Repository of Learning. She had a heavy round body with long, sturdy legs and was covered from head to toe in a thick, wrinkled hide. Her wide elephantine head had two small eyes, two large flat ears, two curved ivory tusks, and a long flexible nose called a trunk. This trunk was a valuable tool, allowing her to reach high tree branches and move the leaves to her mouth, grasp big and small objects, and even communicate with others. Ujuzi served The Animal Kingdom with great compassion and a sense of duty.

Ujuzi the elephant
and Quánwēi the dragon

The gold and white male dragon, named Quánwēi (which means "authority, power, and prestige" in Mandarin), was known as The Keeper of Laws. He had a shining golden-scaled body with a contrasting white-scaled chest. There were a pair of impressive white horns on top of his head, and a long snakelike tail which was also a bright golden color. A pair of leathery dragon wings were connected behind his shoulders and began as a golden yellow at the top, or leading edge. This bright color gradually faded further down the wing, until the transparent material between his wing bones was nearly white. Quánwēi served The Animal Kingdom with gentleness and fair impartiality, a legal phrase referring to equal treatment.

This particular pair of governors were respected by their fellow members of The Animal Kingdom for their honesty, fairness, and problem-solving skills.

The elephant and the dragon lived on opposite sides of a beautiful bowl-shaped valley, along with various other mammals, birds, and reptiles. This sheltered place was known as Governor's Valley. It was located deep inside an immense mountain range, which stretched from the sunrise coastline to the sunset shore of the Earth's single landmass. Tall grasses and flowering bushes bordered a lush green meadow, with brown and red boulders of all shades and sizes scattered throughout the area. Quaking aspens, towering pines, conical fir trees, and fast-growing cottonwoods grew around the verdant pasture. Butterflies and hummingbirds danced skillfully from flower to flower, along with the bees, gathering either nectar or pollen as they went along. There were a few gurgling mountain streams and one long, rushing, rocky river which all fed into a lengthy, narrow lake of sweet, fresh water. This deep-blue rain-fed reservoir filled the low points of the high valley and sat near the center of the meadow. Tall reeds, fast-growing bamboo, and colorful lilies were scattered along the ample shoreline as well as a few sandy beaches, which were perfect for basking in the warm sunlight. Various types of frogs, fish, turtles, and waterfowl enjoyed the lake's freshwater bounty. No additional food or supplies needed to be brought into the area from elsewhere, because the space was its own natural ecosystem.

A great variety of exotic land and air species lived peacefully together inside Governor's Valley. Striped zebras, painted horses, and glittery unicorns danced and played together among the abundant trees and grasses. There were perky meerkats, water-loving capybaras, and trundling porcupines scattered around the valley, with fun-loving monkeys, agile tree kangaroos, sneaky tree snakes, and color-changing chameleons living in the branches above them all. And the skies were filled with swift-flying falcons, flocks of starlings, and fearsome griffins. Due to the incredible diversity gathered in the long bowl-shaped valley, there was quite the variety of individual settlements scattered about the territory. Each site was suited best for the species, so there were dens within the rocks and sand, nests in the trees, and homes dispersed near the water and in the shade of forests.

As you might imagine, Ujuzi the elephant enjoyed roaming the sloping green meadows of the valley with the tall wheat grasses and edible deciduous trees. She liked to stand in the cool, mottled shade among the quiet company of her siblings, sweet nieces, and noisy nephews. Whereas Quánwēi the dragon (as you might also imagine) enjoyed flying around the various tall evergreens which dotted the steep, rocky spaces of the mountain peaks. He liked to spend his evenings inside the damp, craggy cliffs and caves of the mountain face itself, visiting with his fellow cliff-dwellers, his gentle mate, and their young fledglings.

Now, the Earth was still quite young in those days. The world's single landmass was vast and had not yet been torn apart by the planet's plate tectonics. For this reason, The Animal Kingdom enjoyed a single, unbroken supercontinent while the rest of the world was covered in a massive superocean. The vast, salty waters were overseen by The Oceanic Empire and they had their own way of operating, separate from The Animal Kingdom.

The paths of these two governing bodies rarely crossed—except along the coastline, of course—and there was even a third governing body known as The Tidal Realm, which existed to handle disputes along this differing habitat boundary. However, those are separate tales for a separate time.

During the time of this story, there were no battles for territory or food sources being fought upon the great, unbroken landmass. Wars between the various species were rare, though they did erupt occasionally. The many creatures of the earth and the sky were lucky enough to have found a peaceful balance between need and want.

It should also be noted that the number of human beings were few at this point in history, and none had found their way to the protected mountain valley. Most of the Earth's animals kept their distance from the strange-looking, hairless, featherless, scaleless humans, and the humans usually returned the favor. Because of this, the members of The Animal Kingdom were not bothered by mankind very often. Therefore, each and every living beast, either above or upon the land, could still travel wherever they wished on the Earth's single supercontinent—if given enough time, energy, and fortitude. And many did.

Every day, new mammals, birds, and reptiles arrived in Governor's Valley to speak with the elephant and the dragon, hoping for answers or advice in regards to a wide range of topics. Some came for advice on how to resolve a heated dispute between family, friends, or neighbors. Some came to talk through which course to take in life, or how to choose a mate. There were also some who came only to thank the wise governors for the way they had counseled The Animal Kingdom thus far, and perhaps ask for a blessing.

These temporary visitors to the central mountain valley were known as seekers. Seekers journeyed from their homes on every rocky coastline, dusty, sandy desert, verdant plain, wooded vale, towering mountain, and every place in between. Those who were able to fly were able to arrive faster and easier (of course) than those who had to walk or crawl to get there. But, do not worry for those who were born or hatched without wings. There were numerous well-traveled and well-maintained roads across the many plains and forests for the walking beasts, and this allowed the seekers to enjoy the company of their fellow travelers along the way.

When a seeker arrived inside the pristine valley, they would check in with one of the multiple meticulous guardians (you will learn more about them in the next chapter) who kept track of when each seeker arrived. Once they had checked in, the seekers chose a place to set up camp for a night or two, then found something to do while they waited for their turn to talk with the governors. They wandered into the dense forest and walked the trails in the encircling foothills, played in the river, swam in the sparkling lake, and mingled about the entirety of the pristine high mountain vale, visiting with other compatible species.

In the few hours before dusk, after the sun's arc over the valley was done, the nocturnal seekers were given time with the elephant and the dragon. The governors did not want to leave any nighttime animals out of the process simply because their bodies required a different relationship with the path of the sun. So, the governors stayed in place until twilight, the time between sunset and full darkness, which was about the same time that the night guardians to begin the evening watch.

So, when the bright sky had fully darkened over the edge of the tallest mountain ridge, when the crickets and cicadas began their night songs, Governors Ujuzi and Quánwēi would tell the night seekers still gathered near the lake that they would see them the next evening.

"We shall see you all again when the sun brightens the sky again," Ujuzi often called out.

"Yes, and enjoy your evening hours in peace," Quánwēi usually added.

Then the governors bid each other a good night and made their way to their respective homes on opposite ends of the large body of fresh water. Ujuzi returned to her extended family under the generous shade trees which surrounded the grassy meadow around the calm and peaceful lake. Quánwēi returned to the bare, shadowed cliffs behind the forest-rimmed meadow where his mate and fledglings waited for him inside their dark cave roost.

So it was that each day passed beside the water in the beautiful high mountain valley.

CHAPTER 2

At THE BEGINNING OF EACH WORK DAY, Ujuzi the elephant and Quánwēi the dragon arrived from their respective homes on opposite sides of the bowl-shaped valley to meet on the shore of the valley's sparkling lake. There was a long and flat, dark gray rock that extended out into the water from the grassy lakeshore. This natural platform was known as the Seeker's Stone and was the perfect place on which to gather.

After the first meal of the day, but before the first seekers were brought onto the boulder, the elephant and the dragon often enjoyed a private conversation. Most of them went something like this:

"Hello, Quánwēi, how was your evening?" Ujuzi might ask the dragon governor.

"Quite exhausting," Quánwēi might answer, since he and his mate had a clutch of young fledglings at the moment. "The children were restless and did not settle until the moon had set. How was the meadow last night?"

"It was perfect. The sky was clear and the starlight was bright and beautiful," the elephant might answer. "I slept soundly and woke only once to the sound of a night creature laughing. I wondered briefly what was so funny, but sleep overtook me again soon thereafter."

In answer to this, Quánwēi might blow a wisp of smoke and smile his toothy dragon smile before saying something like, "Good for you, my friend. I, myself, miss quiet and peaceful nights. My mate and I will be glad when our fledglings finally grow old enough to sleep through the night, and not accidentally set fire to the bedding material."

"Ah, yes," the elephant might answer wistfully. "I know when my young nieces, nephews, and cousins are having trouble sleeping through the night among the herd. Fortunately, I am able to move away if they are bothering me. I hope it gets better for you soon."

Before long, the first curious creatures of the morning would be led up onto the boulder, to speak with either the elephant or the dragon, and the workday would begin. Each seeker (or group of seekers) was allowed a private audience and given as much time as deemed necessary to resolve an issue or a question. While Ujuzi and Quánwēi spoke with the first seeker, those who were yet waiting would be gathered into a line along the lakeshore and visit quietly with each other while they patiently waited their turn.

The elephant and the dragon spent most of their daylight hours standing or sitting on this boulder, listening to the questions and concerns of those who had traveled so far to speak with them. They both did their best to help their fellow animals by answering questions truthfully and resolving disputes calmly.

Previous wise governors had known that so many different types of birds and animals in one place would eventually cause strife in some form or another. As you can imagine, there was great potential for moments of impatience or misunderstanding between the species waiting to speak with the Animal Kingdom's leaders.

For this reason, there was ever a watchful eye in the sky.

A golden eagle named Aquila (which simply means "eagle" in Italian) was one of the numerous airborne guardians who flew far above the valley meadow every day. He held the important job of watch commander, meaning he was in charge of the other guardians during his working hours. When it was his turn on duty, Aquila spread his long dark-brown and white mottled wings and rode the warm air updrafts until he was soaring high above the beautiful territory. From his lofty view above all the hustle and bustle of the valley, he was able to carefully track the movements of the many and report anything unusual or concerning to other valley guardians down below who were listening for his shrill, whistle-like calls.

Aquila the golden eagle
soaring over the Seeker's Stone

The earthbound guardians were from a diverse group of species too, and lived both around and above the lake, as well as within the shaded forests. There were rabbit, fox, and bobcat guardians; deer, lion, and turkey guardians; and cheetah, wolf, and bear guardians. They all worked collectively to keep the gathered seekers calm and content while they waited to speak with either the elephant or the dragon (as much as possible, that is).

If Aquila the golden eagle was too high up for the valley guardians underneath him to hear his shrill warning calls, a flock of intermediary air messengers were always nearby, listening. These faithful gray and black pigeons were ever at the ready to relay Aquila's concerns to the appropriate ground-based guardian with pigeon coos and even grunting. The guardian would then carefully draw near to the disturbance (or potential disturbance) and watch quietly until they understood the mood of the valley creature in question. After a moment of assessment, the guardian then approached the animal and offered his or her assistance.

It was in this manner that most serious confrontations were avoided, and was the very reason there was peace in the valley—even though it housed many different creatures which should not really get along.

As much as the golden eagle enjoyed his work, he was grateful that the elephant and the dragon were not available to meet with seekers all of the time. A wise old owl from a previous era had advised his own set of governors (which happened to be a tortoise and a raven in those days) to reserve personal time for themselves in order to avoid becoming exhausted under such a heavy social responsibility.

Therefore, it had been decided that every new moon cycle, when the sky was dark for four nights without moonlight shining down upon the land, the reigning leaders should take private time away from meeting with seekers, answering questions, and helping to solve arguments. It was meant to be a time to refresh, meditate, and enjoy their families—a time to play, learn, and rest; a time to feed their weary souls.

Not long after this momentous decision, messenger pigeons were dispatched in pairs to the world's two other equal-but-separate governing bodies—The Oceanic Empire and The Tidal Realm. The messengers shared the old owl's idea of a designated period of rest with the other two sets of leaders, who also chose to implement the restful new moon cycle. Thus, the Earth's land, air, and water creatures all gave themselves time to recover from their labors, and it gave the planet time to rest too.

Aquila was grateful for the wise old owl from a time before, for he was also given a respite from his duties to rest and relax and be with his friends and family.

When mountain-shaded afternoon darkness fell inside the valley, and yet the sky overhead was still bright with the last hours of daylight, most of the residents and seekers made their way back to their individual encampments and their own families for the evening. Aquila the golden eagle turned over the watch command to a great horned owl named Sagesse (meaning "wisdom" in French) before he returned to his neighborhood, leaving the owl to oversee the movements of the nocturnal ones. Included in these nighttime creatures were: clever raccoons, spotted leopards, sneaky foxes, shy aardvarks, wide-eyed bats, and more. When only the moon shone its feeble light down on the valley, these animals visited with each other, swapping stories.

Aquila, himself, spent his time off duty relaxing near the forest. He loved to play with small stones by picking them up with his beak and dropping them at various targets or hunt for supper with his best friends. His chosen home was a bachelor-sized nest on a tall snag, or dead tree, deep in the forest, higher up the mountainside, and well above the peaceful meadow. Most of the other airborne guardians lived deep in the forests, too. Aquila wished to be far from the beautiful valley center when he was not on duty, so he could relax without the noise of so many living beings camping inside the region. He needed his home to be restful, peaceful, and private so he was prepared to do his best work in the coming day.

Do not forget about Aquila the golden eagle. We will check in on him later in this story.

CHAPTER 3

ONE WARM AND CLOUDY SPRING DAY, AS happened plenty of times before, a new creature of The Animal Kingdom had a chance to step onto the wide Seeker's Stone. A curious little brown field mouse named Chota (meaning "small" in Punjabi) had come to talk with Governor Ujuzi and ask her a question.

When it was Chota's turn, the diminutive rodent scurried onto the boulder and boldly approached the big ash gray pachyderm (a scientific word referring to a large mammal with thick skin). Chota rose up on her hind legs and—using her tail for balance—stood as tall and proud as she could. She smiled a toothy smile and spoke in her loudest mousy-voice. "Hello, Governor Ujuzi! It is a great pleasure to *finally* be able to come to Governor's Valley and meet you! My name is Chota, and I have a simple question for you."

Ujuzi smiled her elephant smile, crinkling the thin gray skin around her small eyes, and dipped her large head toward the little mouse as she stood on the boulder. "Hello Chota, it is very nice to meet you as well. Please, ask your question."

"Thank you, Governor Ujuzi. My question is simply this: why do you not have any children yet? You are such a wise and kind leader, I should think it would do The Animal Kingdom a great service if you were to pass along these wonderful traits to future elephantine generations." Here Chota paused to dip her head and frisk her whiskers, then looked up and continued, "I myself have had the privilege of birthing seventy-eight children so far," she squeaked proudly, "and they are all as smart and quick as their Papa."

Now, Ujuzi had heard this question from many others, many times before. She could have easily dismissed the tiny rodent with a wave of her long, flexible trunk and told the minuscule creature to ask this question of someone else, or even to mind her own mousy business. Surely the news of Ujuzi's inability had spread throughout the entire Animal Kingdom by now. Why should she continue to answer such a personal question?

However, the noble pachyderm decided to be merciful and kind with Chota. Perhaps this particular creature had chosen not to pay attention to the global gossip and her question came from a place of genuine curiosity. Therefore, Ujuzi chose to answer the furry brown rodent the same way she had always answered this question.

Graciously, Ujuzi said, "Well, Chota, I have no offspring of my own because, unfortunately, my body is not able to bear children. It was simply not meant for me to be a mother."

"Oh!" squealed Chota as she took a step or two backward, embarrassed. She sat on her hind legs and shook her head, looking to the boulder beneath her. "Now I am sorry to have asked such a question. I hope I have not caused you pain by bringing up such a sore subject. I only meant to . . . to compliment you, really." She hung her head for a moment longer before looking back up to the big elephant. Framed by the thick springtime clouds above her, Ujuzi seemed perfectly regal to the mouse, even though the governors were not really royalty, as such.

Ujuzi smiled sweetly and dipped her head to the side, in an effort to calm the little mammal. "It is all right, Chota," soothed the elephant as she lazily flapped her large fan-shaped ears to cool down. "It is a fair question and I am no longer sad to tell my story. Once I realized that I would never be able to bear calves of my own, I decided to let the dream of motherhood go. I chose to focus on what I *could* do, instead of focusing on what I could *not* do. I reminded myself that I had always been good at learning and retaining even the smallest details, even if they are quite mundane—a word which means 'uninteresting', by the way. Because of this incredible natural gift of a long-term memory, I realized that I could answer a great deal of questions for my friends and family. Therefore, I chose to dedicate my life to serving my fellow fauna by answering their questions, so they, in turn, could live their best lives with less confusion—if they could only learn the answers to what they wished."

The field mouse took a little time to consider Ujuzi's not-so-complicated answer before responding to the governor. She stared down at the ground once again as her nose twitched rapidly from side to side. The light, cool breeze which almost always blew off of the mountain lake suddenly became stronger, and Chota was certain it would rain before too long. She needed to return to her temporary dry nest inside a fallen log soon—but not before she finished her conversation with the elephant.

After a few moments, she looked up at the gentle, long-tusked pachyderm once more and smiled, feeling grateful. "Thank you, Governor Ujuzi," she squeaked.

"You were so kind to me when you did not have to be. Today I have learned that I should not judge others by my idea of how we ought to contribute to our society. Being a mother has been such a wonderful life for me, and it is hard for me to think of another way to live. You are indeed wise. It seems you have chosen your career well, after all. Thank you for your patient answer."

Chota the brown field mouse

"It is my pleasure to serve you, Chota." The elephant smiled as she spoke and lifted her trunk in a friendly goodbye salute. "I hope your days will be a bit sweeter because of this new revelation you have had. I will aspire to live this way as well." Ujuzi smiled to herself, certain Chota would pass this lesson on to her many children. She knew it was best for others to find a conclusion to a difficult question themselves. They tended to remember it longer.

As the little field mouse sat upright, she smiled shyly and tilted her head to one side. "I know you are very busy, Governor . . . but . . . may I ask you *one* more question while I am here?"

"Yes, you most certainly may." Ujuzi slowly lowered her trunk and prepared herself for a potentially difficult matter. However, the small rodent presented an easy question instead.

"What does the word 'fauna' mean?" Chota asked.

Ujuzi chuckled an elephant chuckle, her great, ash gray shoulders jumping slightly before she answered. "Ah, yes. Fauna is another word for animal life. I learned this marvelous word from one of my several teachers many years ago. I think it is one of my favorite words. It is so succinct."

"Oh. Interesting." Chota was not sure what the word 'succinct' meant either (it means "briefly and clearly expressed"), but she did not want to keep the wise governor any longer. She knew time was precious, so she ended her conversation by saying, "I will return home and teach the word 'fauna' to my children, as well as the lesson I have learned today. Perhaps someday they will become as smart as you are, Governor Ujuzi!"

The elephant bowed slightly toward Chota in farewell as the first springtime raindrops fell from the clouds above.

"Very good," Ujuzi answered with a knowing twinkle in her eye. "Your children are fortunate to have such an intelligent mother. Go in peace, my little friend."

CHAPTER 4

ONE BRIGHT SUMMER DAY, AS HAD happened plenty of times before, a new animal had a chance to step onto the Seeker's Stone. A curious large boar named Krepkiy (meaning "strong, robust" in Russian) came to talk with the dragon and ask him a question.

When it was his turn, the massive brownish-black hog sauntered onto the boulder and boldly approached the gold and white firedrake (an Old English word for "dragon"). He stood proudly at attention and spoke in a loud, authoritative voice. "Greetings, Governor Quánwēi. My name is Krepkiy, and it is a great honor to be able to meet you, sir."

Quánwēi smiled his toothy dragon smile, creasing the small golden scales around his lips, and dipped his horned head toward the imposing boar in greeting. He sat his haunches down on the boulder and answered Krepkiy in his deep, smoky baritone. "Hello Krepkiy, it is an honor to meet you as well. Please, ask your question."

"Thank you, sir. My question is this: why have you chosen not to train with the military and go off to help in the territorial wars with the other flying dragons? You are so formidable and obviously quite strong, therefore, I should think you would do The Animal Kingdom a great service if you used your physical power to continue to secure a peaceful future for everyone." Here Krepkiy straightened his bristly spine further and smiled proudly around his upturned tusks before continuing. "I have personally served my local community and helped to keep order and peace in the village for most of my life. It is a good and honorable way to contribute to animal society, as well as the greater good."

Now, Quánwēi had heard this question from many others, many times before. He could have easily dismissed the wild pig with a little snort of dragon fire and told the sizable hairy seeker to ask this question of someone else, or even to mind his own hoggish business. Surely the news of Quánwēi's disability had spread throughout the entire kingdom by now. Why should he continue to answer such a personal question?

However, the scaly golden firedrake decided to be friendly and patient with Krepkiy. Perhaps this particular creature had chosen not to pay attention to the global gossip and his question came from a place of genuine curiosity. Therefore, Quánwēi chose to answer the giant wiry hog the same way he had always answered this question.

Politely, Quánwēi said, "Well, Krepkiy, I am not able to train and fight along with the other dragons because I cannot fly very well. Unfortunately, I hatched with stunted wings which never grew large enough to hold my weight in the air long enough to engage in an air battle."

"Oh," moaned Krepkiy as he dipped his big swine head and shook it slowly back and forth. He was so embarrassed. "I am sorry to have asked you such a personal question, Governor. I hope I have not caused you too much pain by bringing up such a touchy subject. I only meant to compliment you on your obvious physical fortitude."

Quánwēi smiled kindly. "It is all right, Krepkiy," answered the dragon as he scratched an itch on his white-scaled chest with a long talon. "It is a fair question and I am no longer sad to tell my story. Once I understood that I would never be able to fly with my brothers and cousins into battle, I decided to let the dream go. I chose to find another way to keep my fellow animals safe, one which did not test my flying ability. Thankfully—after some frustrating trial and error—I found I had a talent for remembering our many laws and interpreting them carefully. And, as for contributing to society, I am content with the peaceful path I have chosen." Here, he paused to shift his gold and white bulk, and inclined his head toward the pig in a show of appreciation. "I want to thank you for the great work you do to keep your village and community safe, Krepkiy."

Krepkiy the wild boar

The brownish-black boar was surprised by the unexpected gratitude for his choice of profession, especially coming from such a great and respected dragon such as Quánwēi. "Why, thank you for your kindness toward me after my . . . my thoughtless question," he said gratefully. "It seems the career path you have chosen suits you well after all."

Quánwēi bowed his horned golden head toward the bristled wild pig again. "You are quite welcome, my friend. Do you have anything else you would like to talk about while you are here?"

Krepkiy watched the ground, thinking deeply for a moment. He sat on his muscled brownish-black haunches before looking up at Quánwēi again. "As a matter of fact, I think I do have another question. It is something rather baffling that I have been mulling, but was not sure if I should bring the matter before you or go to my community leader. Since I have traveled so far, and you asked me if I had any more questions, I shall ask your opinion on the matter."

The firedrake leaned over to rest his rough, scaly dragon elbows on the boulder and crossed his arms in front of him. "Very well, what is your other question?"

"Well then, do you think it unfair if a parent finds he or she loves one of their offspring a little more than any of the others?" Krepkiy asked before hastily adding,

"I am not asking for myself—oh no—but on behalf of a friend who asked me this very question recently. I spent a lot of time thinking about it. Nonetheless, I could not answer him."

Quánwēi groaned quietly deep inside himself. So many seekers came to the high mountain valley to ask questions which had no true, single answer. Being a creature of The Law himself, Quánwēi generally passed these more philosophical questions on to Governor Ujuzi. But she was quite busy at the moment, sitting patiently on the other side of the Seeker's Stone, helping four turtle sisters work through a heated argument about their shared garden responsibilities.

Since she was clearly too occupied to step away, Quánwēi decided to try and answer the question himself. He shook his golden dragon head slightly in order to clear his thoughts, then looked back down to the wiry boar and said, "Ah, yes. It is an old question, to be sure. Here is my take on the matter, Krepkiy, since I have five adolescent whelps of my own and another clutch of eggs waiting to hatch." Here he paused to blow a puff of smoke from his nostrils up into the air.

Quánwēi continued, "It does not seem possible to control every single sentiment which arises within us, even regarding our children. However, we can work hard at controlling how we react outwardly, regardless of those inner feelings. You may tell your friend this: there is no shame in feeling closer to one child over another in a particular moment, for these emotions will shift and change over time. It is best to work at treating every one of your offspring with the same love, care, and attention as they require from you at the time. Do you understand this, Krepkiy?"

The boar nodded his massive, wiry brownish-black head. "Yes, I believe I do. I will remember your answer and pass this wisdom on to my friend when I return home." Krepkiy stopped to snap to attention once more, and smiled around his upturned tusks. "Thank you very much for sharing your valuable time with me, sir."

Quánwēi closed his golden eyes and bowed his horned head toward Krepkiy one last time. "You are quite welcome. It is my pleasure to serve you and all of my fellow living beings. Go in peace, my friend."

CHAPTER 5

Then, one particularly memorable autumn afternoon, a pair of enormous male tigers came to the elephant and the dragon, asking to speak with both governors at the same time, which was quite uncommon.

When Ujuzi had finished speaking with a kangaroo seeker, a valley guardian informed her of the next appointment. She waited until Quánwēi was done with a group of chimpanzees before stepping over to let the dragon know of the unusual circumstances. The two governors stood side-by-side near the end of the Seeker's Stone, instead of on opposite sides as they usually did, and invited the feline pair onto the stone.

Hinsra (meaning "fierce" in Bengali) and Taamba (meaning "copper" in Hindi) approached the governors upon the boulder slowly and stiffly. Both of their banded tails barely moved and angled toward the ground, showing their agitated mood. These immense cats had traveled from the far side of the mountain range to reach the Governor's Valley and were very, very tired. Needless to say, they were not in very good spirits, either.

Hinsra spoke first, looking up to Quánwēi. "I am Hinsra. My fellow tiger and I cannot seem to agree on which is more important: power or respect. This matter has become a wedge in our friendship, and we can discuss little else as of late. I say *power* is more important, because it gives one the means by which to carry out his or her will—especially in matters of importance. But *he* believes respect is more important, for *some* reason." Hinsra gave a sideways glance and a silent snarl to his fellow tiger, who tried to ignore him.

"Of course power is all well and good," rebutted the second cat quickly, looking at Ujuzi, "but others may choose not to follow those directions, if they do not respect the one giving them." He glanced sideways at Hinsra, ears flat, then back up at the elephant and the dragon. "My name is Taamba," he continued, raising his ears once more, "and we need you both to settle this matter so *he* will know *I* am right after all." This last statement was made with a guttural tiger growl.

Ujuzi and Quánwēi turned their gaze from the pair of fearsome orange and black striped felines and looked at each other instead. A silent moment passed between the elephant and the dragon. It was the kind of moment where two creatures who have known one another for a long time can have a conversation together without saying a single word out loud.

Within this silent moment, it was decided Quánwēi should respond to the seekers first, since he had been addressed by Hinsra first. The gold and white firedrake took a deep breath and let it out slowly, careful not to exhale any flames. He did not want to startle these already anxious tigers.

"Thank you for your challenging question, Hinsra and Taamba," he began slowly, looking at each of them individually as he spoke their names. "The answer you seek may be difficult to understand. My guess is that the two of you are leaders within your shared community back home. Is this correct?"

"Yes," Hinsra and Taamba replied in unison, and with a bit of impatience. The pair had been hoping for a quick answer to their question after so much time debating it between themselves. The dragon's personal inquiry did not bode well for a fast resolution. The tigers both began to sway a bit while they looked up at the towering governors, tails twitching. They transferred their weight from one large front paw to the other, then back again as they swayed. Together they waited for the answer they had traveled so far to receive.

"Very well," answered Quánwēi, noticing their impatient movement with mild unease. He could tell the big tigers were highly agitated and for this reason he tried not to sound too dismissive. Therefore, he decided to begin by complimenting the powerful-looking felines. "It is good for leaders to debate such things. It is good the two of you are each aware of your own strong position on the matter. Both power and respect are important tools for every leader to use."

"Yes, I agree with you. They are both important tools." Hinsra interjected impatiently. "But, we came to ask which is *more* important?"

Quánwēi shook his golden head a little at the imposing tiger and breathed out a thin wisp of smoke before continuing. "Please, have patience. I will answer shortly." He sat his dragon hindquarters on the boulder and turned instead to his pachyderm friend. "Governor Ujuzi, would you please remind us of the differences between the definitions of 'power' and 'respect'?"

"I am always happy to share," replied Ujuzi. She looked from Quánwēi down to the pair of big striped cats and also sat on the Seeker's Stone. She closed her small elephant eyes in order to recall the definitions of the terms better and answered the dragon with her eyes still closed. "Power by itself can be given quickly and taken away quickly by those already in a position of authority. Power can also be forced upon others through the singular will of another, without the others' consent. Power is capable of being wielded by both the competent and the incompetent.

Ujuzi the elephant

"Respect by itself can only be earned over time. It is a positive feeling of admiration, reverence, and honor toward another. Respect is generally wielded by those entrusted with it, those of whom it has been bestowed upon by those around them. The respect of others can be lost, just as with power, though the process is generally slow and usually deserved." As she finished speaking, Ujuzi's small tail swished gently from side to side. She was delighted that she had remembered the two long definitions so perfectly, even though an impatient tiger grumble had almost interrupted her.

When Ujuzi had finished her recitation, she reopened her small elephant eyes and looked back to her longtime dragon friend Quánwēi. It was time for him to share his answer with Hinsra and Taamba.

CHAPTER 6

AQUILA THE WATCH COMMANDER HAD watched from high above when the immense tigers had arrived almost simultaneously, checked in together, then made separate camps near the forest's edge. Neither tiger had chosen to explore the lush, ample territory. Instead, they both paced and grumbled to themselves along the edge of the river, banded tails twitching, and mostly ignored each other. This obvious show of feline agitation concerned Aquila.

The large golden eagle had slowly lowered his altitude above the meadow with wide circles so as not to draw too much attention to himself. When Aquila was flying within hearing range, he could perceive their low growling and heavy breathing as they walked back and forth. These big felines were definitely upset about something—something which had become quite important to them. Something, perhaps, they disagreed upon.

Aquila thought it best to call for ground support to watch the area near the big cats, just in case their barely-buried frustrations erupted into a vicious tiger scuffle. He slowly angled his dark-brown wings to catch the updraft of warm air rising from the ground and circled back up to his normal surveillance altitude. Once there, he called out a series of instructions to those listening for his shrill voice down below.

Odwaga spies the tigress

A great gray wolf named Odwaga (meaning "courage" in Polish) was the first guardian to spring into action after hearing Aquila's whistle-like call. He trotted over to where the massive male cats both paced in separate areas along the rocky river. Each of them had chosen shaded campsites where the waters came out of the forest before winding through the meadow and into the lake. Odwaga lay on a sloping hill in the shade of a great deciduous tree and crossed his large paws in front of him. He watched. And listened. And waited.

Much like Aquila, Odwaga could plainly see the tigers were rather upset. He was grateful to see the two big cats were still keeping a healthy distance—at least for the time being. Just beyond the meadow's reach, not far into the mottled shade of the forest, he noticed a litter of three tiger cubs playing over and around a fallen, moss-covered tree trunk. The children seemed to be enjoying their adventurous trip to the high mountains. He soon spotted their watchful mother lying in the shade between the cavorting cubs and one of the brooding male tigers. The tigress was the picture of calm, yet he was sure there was much contemplation going on behind those green eyes.

The energetic tiger cubs reminded Odwaga of his own litter of triplet wolf pups waiting for him at home. Sometimes it was hard to be away from his family for such long work days, but he knew his mate loved living in Governor's Valley. Nett (meaning "kind" in German) often told him how grateful she was that they were able to live exactly where they did. As he watched, Odwaga was certain his active wolf pups would enjoy having a chance to play with these rambunctious little cubs.

The happy thought of his mate and young ones waiting for him at home caused Odwaga's great wolf-tail to give a single great thump upon the grass, causing the ground to vibrate.

The serene tigress mother heard the noise and turned her piercing gaze toward him.

Odwaga nodded his head once in a friendly greeting.

She nodded back, then returned her attention to her playing children.

As the great gray wolf continued to monitor the male tigers and the playing cubs, he thought it good to stop and rest his body in the tall meadow grasses. The day before, Odwaga had spent the entire afternoon mediating a lakeside territorial dispute between two beavers. Beavers could be very territorial—and rather mean about it.

Just then, a messenger pigeon landed near Odwaga and hopped over to his side. "Watch Commander Aquila sent me to see if there was anything new to report about the recently arrived tigers," she stated, matter-of-factly.

Odwaga glanced again at the big male cats and replied quietly to the gray and black pigeon. "No, there is nothing new at this time. They will probably continue to pace until it is their turn to meet with the governors, and the young children are not a problem. If it looks as if the situation between the males might escalate here at the river's edge, I will give three short howls as a call for help."

"Very good," replied the messenger. She lifted off and flew quickly upward to Aquila in order to deliver his message. She was not the kind of pigeon to waste words.

CHAPTER 7

W HEN IT WAS TIME FOR THE TWO BIG tigers to appear before the elephant and the dragon on the Seeker's Stone, Odwaga the great wolf followed at a discreet distance. He felt he should stay close to the imposing feline pair until the subject which was bothering them had been resolved with the help of the governors. With this much obvious tension between such big cats, he knew what might happen if one or both of them received an answer they were not pleased with.

Odwaga sat on a gentle slope of grass near the wide, flat Seeker's Stone and listened to the discussion while looking out over the lake. His nose twitched as he smelled the breeze which was filled with the rich fragrance of countless plants and living beings.

By now another valley guardian, a female black bear named Yona (which simply means "bear" in Cherokee), had also heard the warning call from Aquila the eagle. From a distance, she had seen Odwaga carefully follow the immense felines to the boulder, and she decided to sit near the elephant and the dragon, too.

"Good day, Odwaga," said Yona as she settled next to him with a bear-sized grunt. She also gazed out over the calm and peaceful lake, taking in the beauty. "It sure is a pleasant one. I think these two tigers are the most interesting case the valley has had all week long."

"Good day, Yona," answered Odwaga quietly. "I believe you are right. Before these two big cats started pacing, the most interesting case of the day—that I know of—was a blind raccoon who accidentally wandered into Saltador the rabbit's private vegetable garden." (Saltador is the Spanish word for "jumper".)

Yona imagined a frustrated look on Saltador's face, his long ears quivering rapidly, as the blind raccoon shook his head in embarrassed remorse. Her great bear-bulk bounced as she chuckled softly at the thought. "I missed that one. I must have been off helping the aging giraffes on the sunrise side of the meadow pluck leaves from the higher branches." She stopped speaking, transferred her weight to her left hip, stuck out her right leg and sighed with contentment. "It has been a rather dull day until now," she said.

A brightly colored butterfly danced and flitted into view before it alighted on one of Yona's curved toe claws. Yona and Odwaga watched it quietly together as it folded and unfolded its orange and black wings before flying off to a nearby cluster of white daisies.

Odwaga the great gray wolf
and Yona the black bear

"I am grateful for dull days," mused Odwaga once the butterfly was out of view. "They give me time to ponder." He shifted his gaze to the oversized lake boulder. Those tigers still seemed mighty upset to him. They were both swaying impatiently now, shifting their weight from one great paw to the other, back and forth, back and forth. Odwaga carefully judged the distance it would take for him to jump up there, if it looked like he might need to intervene.

Yona scrunched up her long, black nose and regarded the oversized canine sitting beside her. "Ponder? What kind of things does a wolf need to ponder in a peaceful territory such as this?"

"Probably much of the same things a bear ponders." He turned his head to look back at her. "Things like my den, my mate, and my cubs; if I am doing enough for them. Things like the coming frost season; if we will be ready by the time the first snowflakes tumble down from the clouds. Things like what kind of unforeseen troubles might arise tomorrow; and if we are prepared for the worst of it."

"Yes," replied Yona with another heavy sigh. "I suppose I think about those things a lot, too."

The valley guardians turned their respective gazes to the forest view across the lake as they listened to birdsong and the discussion taking place on the Seeker's Stone. The gray wolf and the black bear fell into a comfortable silence beside each other as they watched the many beasts, birds, and reptiles graze or play around the meadow and lake shore. For the moment, they were simply two large forest animals enjoying a quiet moment together by the shore of a high mountain valley lake.

After a bit, Odwaga and Yona returned their full attention back to the nearby boulder on which the elephant and the dragon and the tigers were having a long conversation.

CHAPTER 8

AFTER UJUZI HAD FINISHED RECITING THE definitions of power and respect, Quánwēi the dragon looked back down to the swaying pair of anxious tigers. "Do you understand the differences between these two words as they have been defined to you?" he asked the seekers in his smoky dragon baritone.

"Yes," said Hinsra and Taamba simultaneously as they continued to rock back and forth, tails twitching. Their ears were pinned back and their faces wore twin tiger frowns. They were still waiting to see which one of them was right, and the long, drawn-out definitions from the elephant were an unwelcome delay.

Quánwēi smiled before continuing, hoping to relax the felines with his friendliness, and crossed his arms.

"Good. You see, the understanding of respectful authority is influenced by many things, namely the assumed integrity of the respected one. In contrast, the understanding of forced authority is generally influenced only by the fear of the one under the thumb of forced authority. Authority gained through fear tends to be a weak and temporary power when compared to respect." Here, Quánwēi became caught up in the ideas of his teaching and moved a scaly claw in small circles as he spoke. "Therefore, the best answer to your question, Hinsra and Taamba, is this." Here he paused to look at each of them carefully. "Respect tends to be the most influential form of power. Once you have the respect of those under your command, your words will have the strength you wish them to have. Having said that, you must earn respect with your integrity, which means 'living honestly'. Do you both understand this?"

Taamba answered Quánwēi first, though he glared directly at his fellow tiger while speaking to the firedrake. "Yes, sir. I understand my opinion is the correct one. You said that *respect* is more influential, and therefore more important, than power alone."

Hinsra growled at the words of Taamba and spat out his own words as he turned to face his friend, "No, you were not listening, Taamba. The dragon told us that respect is only a *form* of power. So *power* is the true answer."

Taamba growled back.

Now the two tigers began pacing back and forth across the boulder in feline frustration. It did not sound to either them like the gold and white dragon had given an easy solution to their very important, very aggravating disagreement. Hinsra and Taamba walked the entire width of the boulder in opposite directions in front of the two governors. Each time the tigers passed one another, they bared their teeth, mouths wide, and hissed loudly.

Hinsra and Taamba the tigers

Ujuzi and Quánwēi were not surprised by this dramatic reaction from this pair of seekers. They had seen this type of stress-induced response from other animals who had argued over a particular issue for many days. All of their long-repressed, aggressive emotions still needed to be released, and usually came out as some kind of physical movement.

At this point in the story, Odwaga the great wolf and Yona the black bear stepped cautiously from the gentle, grassy slope and moved toward the Seeker's Stone entrance. Their quiet moment staring across the lake watching ducks, beavers, and moose play in the water was now over. Both guardians felt the need of their enforcing presence near the governors.

When Odwaga and Yona stepped forward, the ferocious cats stopped pacing—briefly. Yet they were not impressed for long. After a blink or two, they both began pacing across the boulder once more.

Ujuzi and Quánwēi nodded to the imposing pair of valley guardians in order to acknowledge their protective company, then returned their attention to the anxiously pacing cats.

The pachyderm was concerned, and spoke to the pair, saying, "It seems you are both still confused. Perhaps we have not been clear. What Governor Quánwēi was *trying* to relay is this: power and respect are equally important. It is best if you use them simultaneously."

Hinsra and Taamba both continued to glower and pace, showing no outward sign they had heard her words.

Ujuzi continued, "Please listen, my friends. Ideally, those with elected authority should have already earned the respect of those around them; those over whom they supervise. And, let me say this as carefully as I can." She paused, gazed up to the slow-moving clouds and swished at a fly with her tail before continuing. "We should all remember that we need not be in an official leadership position in order to have our decisions be noticed by those who already respect us." She returned her attention back to the tigers. "We should all seek to live rightly, knowing that our choices may have an impact on others—regardless of our community position."

The tigers continued to glower and pace, but Taamba moved at a slower speed than before. The elephant and the dragon could see that at least one big cat was beginning to figure it out.

Nevertheless, Ujuzi had become impatient with the pair of frustrated felines. "Please. Listen to me," she said, taking a single step toward them in her eagerness to help them understand.

The large cats were startled by her movement for a moment and glanced up at her as their pacing faltered.

Ujuzi continued in a softer voice. "Governor Quánwēi and I are trying to convey that power and respect are *equally* important and should be wielded together. They should not be separate entities."

Both tigers finally stopped their pacing. They were now still, but stood as far from one another on the boulder as they could. They each looked up at the elephant and the dragon once more.

"So . . . you are saying we are *both* right?" asked Hinsra, his ears still very flat upon his head, his banded tail lashing savagely side to side.

"They are equally important?" asked Taamba, his ears beginning to rise, his tail now hanging loosely.

"Yes," said Ujuzi and Quánwēi at the same time. The governors began to relax. The tigers finally understood.

Quánwēi took the teaching moment a little further. "You know, you are both right, in a way. If you had come to ask us if power was important—the answer would have been 'yes.' If you had come to ask us if respect was important—the answer would have been 'yes.' But you came to ask which one was more important. The answer to that is actually 'neither', because they are equally important.

"Just because a friend does not agree exactly one hundred percent with your point of view does not mean he or she is wrong. There are *many* matters in which it is perfectly all right to have different opinions."

Taamba the tiger sat and gazed out over the lake, seeing its beauty for the first time now that his mind was not so anxious. He no longer felt the need to pace. He understood what the elephant and the dragon were saying. He felt embarrassed and ashamed that he had let the bitter argument go on so long with his friend, neighbor, and fellow community leader.

However, Hinsra did not choose to sit and relax. Not yet. He looked up to Quánwēi and said, "You said that respect is a power, therefore power is the answer— the *only* answer." He faced his fellow community leader. "So *I* am right, Taamba. You should not have disagreed with me."

The elephant and the dragon could not help it, they both sighed loudly. This was not going well after all.

Taamba was a little surprised by Hinsra's continued negative attitude. "I am allowed my own opinion on the matter," he answered defensively, but not angrily. "I happen to agree with the two governors we have come so far to seek advice from. I believe we are both wrong and we are both right." He shook his tiger head and quietly added, "You do not have to be so arrogant about it all, Hinsra."

Hinsra did not like that statement. Not at all. He arched his back, flattened his ears against his head, and lunged at Taamba with his teeth bared and long tiger claws extended.

Yona the bear had anticipated this reaction. She also charged forward and placed herself directly between the two immense felines.

CHAPTER 9

AT THE VERY MOMENT YONA MOVED, Odwaga the great gray wolf moved too. But instead of heading for the space between the tigers, Odwaga leapt over the seekers and landed between the elephant and the dragon. He turned around, head low, and took a defensive posture slightly forward of the governors. He faced the big striped cats without fear. Odwaga was ready to protect the elephant and the dragon if Hinsra decided to go after either of them next.

However, the sudden show of protective strength from the two valley guardians startled Hinsra. He backed away from Taamba and the black bear immediately, though his ears were still as flat as they could be. Hinsra could not bring himself to look at Taamba, or the elephant and the dragon, or the two newcomers, choosing instead to stare at the surface of the boulder. Deep down inside, Hinsra still believed he was right and Taamba was wrong, and he needed someone to acknowledge that fact out loud. He still felt his fellow feline had wronged him, somehow, by disagreeing with him so strongly.

Taamba had not moved. Sitting on the flat boulder, he gazed forlornly at his friend, neighbor, and fellow leader. Sadly he asked, "Is our friendship now lost? Must it be lost because of this one disagreement?"

Hinsra continued to stare at the boulder, intentionally avoiding eye contact with his longtime friend. His shoulders slumped and he let out a long, frustrated tiger sigh. He had said all he had come to say, and had no more words for Taamba. Hinsra slowly turned around without looking at his former friend, or the governors, or the guardians. He walked off of the Seeker's Stone, onto the grassy shore of the lake, and slunk sluggishly back to the forest—alone this time. He followed the same path he and Taamba had taken together to the lakeside boulder, shaking his head, muttering to himself.

The five creatures remaining upon the boulder mournfully watched him go, their collective grief evident. The elephant and the dragon grieved inwardly at the tigers' loss of friendship. The guardians, Odwaga and Yona, shook their heads sadly, too.

Taamba the tiger sat forlornly, his shoulders were slumped, his head hung low. He looked at the black bear through humble eyes and spoke quietly. "Thank you. Thank you for being willing to step between us, to protect us from each other. I regret that I let our argument get so heated and cause such strong feelings. I am sorry for . . . for all of this." He closed his eyes in remorse.

Yona answered, "You are welcome." She then turned her attention to the governors. "I will follow after Hinsra and see to it that he makes no further trouble on his way out of Governor's Valley." She dipped her head in a respectful bow to Ujuzi and Quánwēi before carefully following behind the sulking tiger.

Taamba continued to sit downcast before the elephant and the dragon and the wolf. He was in no hurry to leave their presence. He was suddenly unsure of what to do, or where to go.

Quánwēi spoke to the remaining big cat with sadness in his voice. "It appears you have lost a long friendship over this disagreement of words and definitions. My condolences."

Taamba looked sadly up at him.

Quánwēi lowered his horned head close to Taamba and spoke softly. "Even though things did not go well for you, I believe you have acted honorably and with a respectable show of social manners. You are wiser now than when you arrived in the valley, Taamba. I can see your mind is open to change."

Taamba simply sighed again in response.

Quánwēi the dragon

The firedrake glanced over at Ujuzi to ask her another question without using words. The pachyderm nodded her ash gray head at Quánwēi, her long ivory tusks moving near his golden-scaled head. He turned his gaze back to the single seeker and continued. "Taamba, Governor Ujuzi and I wish to offer you a position here in the protected vale—as a Valley Guardian."

Taamba stared agape at the dragon before stuttering, "I . . . I . . . ," before falling silent again. After a moment's consideration, he said, "Yes. I humbly accept. My mate and I have been discussing making a change, and from her comments when we first arrived here, I believe she would love to stay."

Odwaga the great wolf guardian stepped forward and addressed governor Quánwēi before he had time to respond. "Sir, since this tiger brought his mate and cubs along with him on the journey, they will want to find a home quickly. I know an area in the forest near my home where Taamba could make a nice den. I believe our children are of similar age and might become friends, if given the chance. Also, if it pleases my governors, I should like the opportunity to instruct Taamba in the administrative ways of Governor's Valley."

The gold and white dragon nodded appreciatively at the gray wolf. "Thank you for your offer, Guardian Odwaga. I believe your natural gift of patience would make you an excellent instructor," Quánwēi said. Turning back to the glum feline, he asked, "Does this seem like a reasonable plan to you?"

Taamba, still seated, blinked a few times before answering. He could hardly believe they really wanted him to stay after such a disastrous meeting. "Yes, I think it does. You see, Hinsra and I have shared the leadership responsibilities in our large jungle community for a long time, and I am certain he does not want me to return with him to our village. The journey here together was difficult enough—very awkward and full of frustrating conversations. There is far too much tension between us now. I cannot imagine he would allow me to live in peace near him any longer."

Ujuzi, Quánwēi, and Odwaga all bowed their heads toward Taamba in a show of appreciation for his choice to join them.

"Welcome to the valley, Guardian Taamba," the elephant and the dragon said in unison.

"We look forward to what you have to teach us and hope we can all be good neighbors," added Ujuzi. She raised her long trunk in a salute before adding the customary blessing. "May you and your family grow strong and healthy in this peaceful mountain territory."

Taamba stood and bowed low as a respectful thank you to the leaders of The Animal Kingdom. He was grateful to be accepted by the governors and the great gray wolf.

"Come," said Odwaga as he took a few steps toward the forest. "I will walk back with you to your tigress and cubs. Along the way I will share what I can about how the guardian command structure functions here in the valley. After that, I would like to introduce your family to mine. Nett, my mate, will be pleased to have another female friend to confide with on matters of motherhood."

The wolf and the tiger stepped off of the Seeker's Stone together and headed to the place where the river emerged from the forest. Odwaga spoke in a low voice as they walked along, teaching the new guardian the basics of valley life.

Ujuzi and Quánwēi shared a long, wordless look before she said, "That was quite difficult. I am glad such cases do not come to us very often."

Quánwēi agreed with a nod, and blew out a little smoke from his nostrils to calm himself down. "I agree, my friend. The meeting did not end successfully, but we tried our best. Sometimes seekers are simply not willing to listen to our advice. However, I believe we have added a good soul to the ranks of the valley guardians today." He waved a waiting messenger pigeon over to his side and told her of the new feline guardian and his family as she sat on his shoulder.

Once the information was relayed, the air messenger joined her fellow pigeons grouped near the tall grasses beside the lake. She shared the news of the new tiger guardian and pointed him out to the others, whereupon the flock scattered to share the latest information with the rest of the valley guardians. She then flew up, high over the lake and delivered the news to Watch Commander Aquila, too.

So it was that the peaceful mountain meadow gained a new, permanent resident guardian that day.

CHAPTER 10

With SHARP EYES, THE GOLDEN EAGLE watched the big cat drama unfold from high above the bowl-shaped mountain meadow. Aquila could not hear the words of the elephant and the dragon and the tigers from his soaring altitude, but he could imagine it. The two large felines were pacing, clearly agitated, yet the watch commander was not worried. Odwaga and Yona were both skilled, respected, and experienced guardians, so he was confident they could help settle any matter if things became physically confrontational between the agitated tigers.

Aquila continued to circle, monitoring the entire valley below as the various guardians went about their work. It was always calming to observe a herd of antelope graze near the lake, or a school of fish swim inside the sparkling lake, or adventurous young griffins exploring the branches near their family's large nest of branches. Governor's Valley was such a beautifully diverse community and he never tired of seeing each of the creatures go about their day. He had to be careful not to be distracted while still on duty, though, especially since he was watch commander.

So, Aquila focused his attention to the other side of the mountain lake, where a tall bull moose guardian named Tarn (meaning "tower" in Norwegian), was attentively checking in on a first-time fox mother and her just-arrived brood of kits. Aquila knew Tarn would make certain the little furry group was well taken care of during their new family experience.

Seeing movement from the wide Seeker's Stone beside the lake, the golden eagle watched as one tiger left the stone and angled back toward his camp on the edge of the forest. Yona the black bear soon followed him at a discrete distance. Shortly after, the other big cat was escorted by Odwaga the great wolf from the Seeker's Stone. They, too, moved slowly back to the periphery of the trees, keeping a healthy distance from the first tiger. Aquila could tell from the way their heads stayed close together that they were clearly discussing something. The golden eagle wondered what distressing thing had transpired for the two tigers to have left the stone separately when they had arrived in the valley together.

Aquila did not have to wonder very long, though, for he soon spotted a messenger pigeon on her way up to him, her black and gray wings flapping wildly. Between great, gulping breaths the pigeon shared her news regarding the longtime disagreement which had brought the big cats to the governors, the ensuing argument, and the fact that one of the felines would be staying in the valley with his family as a new guardian.

Ah, Aquila thought to himself as she flew away, *that explains the curious way they left the governors.* The golden eagle found he was looking forward to meeting this Taamba the tiger. From what the pigeon had shared, it seemed as if the feline newcomer would be eager to learn, grow, and contribute to their peaceful life in the valley.

The shortened autumn day was drawing to a slow end. Aquila could see the bright afternoon sun creeping closer to the rim of the tall mountain range, with the shadows growing ever longer on the ground far below him. It was almost time for the changing of the watch, and he turned his head just in time to see Sagesse the great horned owl approaching.

"Good day, Aquila," the mottled brown and white owl said in greeting. "I just heard the news of the tigers, have you?"

"Yes," Aquila answered. "I heard emotions were intense on the boulder for a while. Apparently the two seekers could not agree to disagree without hard feelings."

Sagesse nodded as he flew gracefully next to the eagle. "Well, regardless, I think it will be good to have another ground guardian join us on the night watch. I hope to meet the new tiger and his family tonight, as tigers are mostly nocturnal."

Aquila already knew this fact, but kept his thoughts to himself. "Yes, my friend, it is always good to have more help with our work," he said politely. "Now, I officially transfer the watch commander duties to you, my friend, and wish you a good evening."

"Thank you. Sleep well, Aquila. I will see you in the morning."

At this, the golden eagle veered off from the owl and angled toward his tall tree snag deep in the forest. He knew nighttime in the mountain meadow, forests, and encircling foothills would be well taken care of by the owl, puma, hedgehog—and now tiger—guardians. They would watch carefully over the movements of the other nocturnal creatures from dusk until dawn, while Aquila slept soundly in his bachelor's nest, recharging for the next day's work.

Aquila the golden eagle

The sunset side of the valley was already dark in the mountain's long shadow and he could hear the crickets and cicadas beginning their rhythmic night songs. An early evening fog gathered in an ethereal mist over the lake below and he watched as the valley was blanketed in early twilight. The governors had already begun meeting with the nighttime seekers and would soon be done for the day.

As Aquila flew home, he knew the light of early morning might bring old challenges, new concerns, and innovative resolutions. Nonetheless, with the help of each and every guardian, the beautiful mountain valley would likely continue to be a safe haven for all of those who came to seek an audience with the elephant and the dragon.

THE END

Make this author happy today!

If you enjoyed my book, please consider posting a

review. Even if it's only a single sentence, it

would be a huge help.

PRONUNCIATION OF CHARACTER NAMES

(in alphabetical order)

CHARACTER	ORIGIN	PRONUNCIATION
AQUILA the golden eagle	Italian	ə-kwi-lə (UH-kwee-luh)
CHOTA the field mouse	Punjabi	chōtə (CHO-tuh)
HINSRA the tiger	Bengali	hēn-shü (HIN-shoo)
KREPKIY the wild boar	Russian	ckrē-ep-kē (Kr-EP-key)
NETT the great wolf	German	net (N-et)
ODWAGA the great wolf	Polish	ōd-vä-gə (Odd-VAH-guh)

QUÁNWĒI the dragon	Mandarin Chinese	chen-wā (Chen-WAY)
SAGESSE the horned owl	French	saʒɛs (SAAH-zhez)
SALTADOR the rabbit	Spanish	sȯl-tä-dȯrr (Sal-TA-doorr)
TAAMBA the tiger	Hindi	täm-bä (TOM-bah)
TARN the moose	Norwegian	tärn (T-AR-n)
UJUZI the elephant	Swahili	u-jü-zē (Ooo-JU-zee)
YONA the black bear	Cherokee	yō nə (YO-nuh)

ACKNOWLEDGMENTS

AS MY FIRST PUBLISHED BOOK, this little fable will always be dear to me, as are the people who encouraged me to pursue Adventures in Writing.

My parents, Greg and Anne, instilled a love of reading into my older sister and I. They read classics like C.S. Lewis' Narnia Series and J.R.R. Tolkien's *The Hobbit* out loud to us. They even took turns with narration and assigned each character a voice as they read. I know how fortunate we were to have this kind of introduction to literature and story. My active imagination had no problem setting the scene as the book played out like a movie in my head.

Gratefully, my parents showed no fear or disdain at my choice to write fiction. Being creative people themselves, my foray into authorship may even have seemed natural to them, probably because of their shared love of reading.

I want to thank my father in particular, for providing the animal sketches in this fable. He was always doodling on scrap paper when I was growing up, particularly while he was trapped in a chair, talking on a corded home phone. When I asked him if he'd be willing to sketch the characters for this fable, I think he was flabbergasted. Sometimes we don't see our own talents clearly until we allow an outside perspective into our private insecurities. (Your drawings are great, Dad, all the beta readers said so.)

Thank you to my sister, Julie, and her husband and children for reading the earliest drafts of this story and still offering support.

Since I've added these acknowledgments in a later edition of the fable, I would also like to thank the eagle-eyed members of my writer's critique group: Barb, Barbara, Denise, Jenna, and Pete, as well as Wendi and Jenna. They all paid attention to the intended voice of the story and their offered suggestions helped to make the story read more clearly—more linear—than the first edition.

And last, but certainly not least, I thank my husband, Eddie. Though fiction (and reading in general) are not his idea of a good time, he still supports me. He encourages me to keep pushing, keep learning, keep honing my craft—and that, my friends, is invaluable.

This fable is a much better story due to the invaluable feedback I've received from each and every one of these generous people.

Thank you!

88 CS SIMPSON

Also by CS Simpson

The Fable Triad:

The Elephant and the Dragon
The Dolphin and the Octopus
The Mermaid and the River Otter

About the Author

CS Simpson is a multi-genre writer of several short stories, some poetry, and a novel. Her work can be found in Shoreline of Infinity, the Pikes Peak Writers Anthologies, frontiertales.com, and her own self-published fables. When she's not writing, editing, or stressing about writing, she's either devouring other author's books or playing The Sims and watching movies while sipping Diet Coke. She also enjoys short hikes with her husband and dog under the Colorado skies she calls home.

Keep up with her writing journey at www.authorcssimpson.com

About the Publisher

CSS Stories is the self-publishing line of fictional tales by author CS Simpson.

94 CS SIMPSON

www.ingramcontent.com/pod-product-compliance
Lightning Source LLC
Chambersburg PA
CBHW021017160726
47994CB00006B/2550